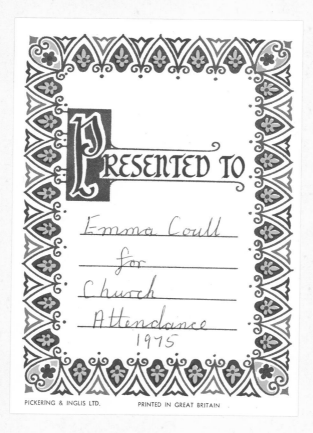

PRESENTED TO

Emma Coull

for

Church

Attendance

1975

PICKERING & INGLIS LTD.   PRINTED IN GREAT BRITAIN

THE MUSIC-MAKERS

THE MUSIC-MAKERS

by

P. CATHERINE COLES

VICTORY PRESS

EASTBOURNE

© VICTORY PRESS 1974

ISBN 0 85476 209 4

Printed in Great Britain for
VICTORY PRESS (Evangelical Publishers Ltd.),
Lottbridge Drove, Eastbourne, Sussex,
by Richard Clay (The Chaucer Press) Ltd.,
Bungay, Suffolk.

CONTENTS

FIRST IMPRESSIONS

When the rumour spread through the town that Beechwood House was sold it started endless speculation. Who, in their right minds, could possibly have bought it?

Beechwood House was the last relic of the fine old Beechwood Estate. The mansion house itself had disintegrated through neglect, and the fact that high prices made repairs and upkeep impossible. The grounds had long been taken over, sold to a private firm of house builders, to pay off death duties; and now, where once there had been beautifully kept lawns and borders, magnificent azaleas and rhododendrons, there were rows and rows of modern box-like bungalows with neat but unexciting gardens.

Beechwood House was an awkward reminder of better days. It had been a fine house in its prime, somewhere between the mansion house and the cosy lodges that had stood guard at the main gates. Even so, by present day standards it was a white elephant. It lacked the grace and architectural beauty of the mansion house but was solid and square in old grey stone. It had seven bedrooms and three public rooms, a huge stone-flagged kitchen, and fully an acre of ground still clung around it, much as a child shyly clings to its mother's skirts in the presence of strangers. The house was too big for a twentieth-century family, too small for a hotel, too unsuitable for a nursing home. So it had lain cobwebby and disconsolate for five years.

And now it was sold! The workmen who had been

employed to put it in some semblance of habitable order could offer few solid facts for the neighbours to build on. The alterations were minimal, considering the state it was in, so the curious had to wait and see, and they used the time inventing the most unlikely solutions to the mystery.

The removal vans arrived on a sunny Saturday morning in March, and only the very indifferent could resist standing to stare when a third and then a fourth van disgorged furniture, carpets, crates and boxes. As the vans only bore the name of a well-known removal firm with branch depots all over the country, there was not even the crumb of information as to where the newcomers had come from. A tall man had preceded the vans in a small green car and had been about the place all day, obviously directing operations. Then there had been a fair-haired girl of about fifteen or sixteen who had come with him and who seemed to have all the domestic side of a removal wonderfully under control.

Then about half past four a large blue and white Dormobile drew up in a nearby road. The driver, a lean, pleasant-looking lad, checked his whereabouts on a small map, drove up the remains of the old Beechwood drive and disappeared out of sight between the tall trees. It still wasn't much to go on, but in those brief moments while the car was halted it had been possible for bystanders to count no fewer than seven heads, and all but one were children, apart from the driver who could be anything from seventeen to twenty.

A school? A 'home'? Whatever else could bring nine people—and that number grew considerably as the snippet of news was passed verbally at the street corner or by telephone.

The vehicle pulled up at the rear of the house, so no

one saw the most worthwhile sight that would have
kept the tongues wagging all night. The lean lad
jumped down from the driver's seat and went round
to the side nearest the house.

"Hi, Dad! Hi, Sue! We've made it!" he called, as
he swung open the side doors. Out tumbled the family. Four excited children rushed into the house and
a motherly looking woman stepped out after them.
The man who had been around all day strode over
to welcome her and then disappeared inside the car.
When he came out again a few seconds later he was
carefully manipulating a wheelchair. The lad then
took one side, and together the chair and its young
occupant were set safely on the ground.

"Hullo, Kitten! Had a good run?"

"Yes, Daddy!"

The spastic child nodded, her face alight with the
same excitement as the rest, her arms held out to be
picked up and carried into the house to see for herself
all the wonders of their new home.

"Come on in. Sue's done wonders in the kitchen
and there's a very good meal just about ready by the
sounds and the smells from that quarter."

A few minutes later the door was shut and all was
quiet on the outside though there was plenty of noise
ringing round the kitchen as the family took their
first meal there. The next hour passed with eating and
recovering from the day's exertions and then in that
first exciting exploration of finding old treasures set
in new surroundings.

Presently the back door opened again and the lean
lad and the fair-haired Sue came running out hand in
hand, laughing and chaffing each other. They swung
open the big side doors of the Dormobile and Sue
dived inside. When she emerged she was carrying a
cello.

"Take this first, Colin, and I'll get the rest of the stuff ready. Give Tony and Pete a shout."

Colin took the big instrument with the care of long practice, and went indoors.

"Tony! Peter! Props to shift!"

His clear voice rang out through the uncarpeted house.

Two boys in jeans and Arran sweaters tumbled out of the house together.

"Careful!" Sue admonished. "Here, Tony, you take the two fiddles; and, Peter, take this box of stands and things. Put them in the room to the right of the front door. You'll see 'Cleopatra' there. Put things down safely where we shan't fall over them."

'Cleopatra', for no known reason, was the name given years ago to the old family piano.

Colin was back first and went in again with a record-player. Then the younger boys carried in boxes of records, stacks of music, and a variety of smaller instruments.

"How are you doing, Sue?" a voice called from an upper window.

"Fine thanks, Dad. Just a few of Mary's things, and that's the lot."

Later that evening one local man got the surprise of his life. Constable Shepherd was a conscientious policeman and kept a good watch on his district. He was also a very kindly man. He had heard that the new people were arriving at Beechwood that day and he, too, had wondered about them. 'Strangers in a strange land', he called them, speaking to his wife as he prepared to go on his late night round. He decided to take a turn up the old drive to what he considered to be a barn of a place and just satisfy himself that all was well with the newcomers. The big house was in darkness except for a light in the hall and in one uncurtained room beside the front door. Constable Shepherd pulled up his car a short distance from the house and switched off the engine. At once he was arrested by the sound of music. The window was open a little and he stood, unashamedly listening and watching the unusual scene.

A man was playing the piano, nearby a woman and a boy were playing violins, a girl held a cello and another boy a flute. Two young ones were playing recorders and—yes, he had to believe his own eyes though he would have found it hard to accept on any-one else's telling—there was a small girl in a wheel-chair beating time on a triangle. Spellbound, the man listened as the family sang and played together.

"Well! A whole box of musical tricks all to themselves!"

Constable Shepherd drove slowly away. They did not seem to need him and his kind enquiries at the moment. As he went, for some reason he could not fathom he felt more moved than he had done for many a day. A torn luggage label lay at the side of the drive; he stopped and picked it up. It read: 'J. Baird and family, Beechwood House, Middlebridge.' He drove on again, skilfully avoiding Mrs Cooper's black cat that would sit in the gutter outside her house. As he garaged the car he regretted that his position pro-hibited him from broadcasting this choice item of news. As it was, he could share it with his wife Jean who was the soul of discretion. He locked up and went indoors. He had a strong feeling that the coming of the Bairds was going to make a most unusual impression on Middlebridge.

CHAPTER TWO

FRIENDS AND NEIGHBOURS

Mrs Cooper was the first to see the new family, and she could hardly believe it when she saw them. From her seat just behind her curtains in her corner bungalow she got a good view up and down the road and across to the end of the old drive, where it joined the road through the new Beechwood Housing Scheme.

On Sunday morning she was suddenly aware of a man and a woman whom she had never seen before coming towards her house. There were two children with them: a girl of about seven and a boy she guessed to be a bit older. They were carefully dressed, and obviously going to church.

"So!" observed the old woman to herself.

As they passed on down the road, Mrs Cooper's attention was drawn to two boys in the casual clothes of the modern youth. Both were scrupulously clean and tidy and they, also, were obviously making for the church. Behind them came a tall boy with an equally tall girl beside him. Both were good-looking, and Mrs Cooper judged that the girl must be about sixteen and the boy eighteen or nineteen. But, apart from a quick summing up of these two, her interest was given to the little figure in a wheelchair, being pushed by the lad. The child was fair and very thin, almost elf-like in looks, and she was pointing and laughing at Mrs Cooper's cat curled in its usual place at the roadside.

Instinctively Mrs Cooper dropped the corner of the curtain back into place. She loved to spy on the comings and goings of her near neighbours, but she had a sense of decency, for all her spying was harmless curiosity born out of her lonely widowhood. For a second she was tempted to put on her coat and hat and rush out to join the church-going cavalcade. The very sight of that family had touched an old chord in her memory. Once she had gone to all the services regularly: as a child, as a youngster, as a bride and as a mother. But with the passage of time she had drifted away and on coming to a new area she had never made the effort to start again. But she couldn't follow the strangers on impulse—what would the neighbours think? Well she knew: she could just hear Mrs Hill saying, 'Now where's that old Curiosity Cat off to?'

She turned away and tried to concentrate her thoughts on the small mundane affairs of her unimportant household. She switched on the radio and forced herself to listen to the urbane voice that had no power to hold her. She kept glancing at the clock. She *must* reassure herself by the sight of their return that the family were real and that she hadn't been 'seeing things'.

Quite unaware of the effect they had had on their unknown neighbour, the Bairds walked on and presently they were causing looks of pleased surprise as they made their way into the church built on the corner of the cross-roads. They filled up a whole pew and overflowed into the one behind. Everything about the service was familiar to them and they joined in the worship wholeheartedly. As they were sitting at the back and to the side to accommodate the wheelchair, they were able to enjoy the service undisturbed, for the congregation, in spite of burning curiosity, were too well-mannered to turn round and stare.

Mr Thompson, the minister, was at the door to greet them as they filed out and was soon introducing them to his wife, who promptly invited them all for tea that afternoon. As she did so, she was rapidly counting heads and mentally reviewing her reserve store-cupboard. The Bairds tried to refuse, not because they did not want to go but to prevent the Thompsons having so large an invasion at such short notice. But it was no use; they would accept no refusal.

Over lunch Mrs Thompson was still occupied with store-cupboard thoughts, her husband was beaming over the letter he had been given from the Baird's previous minister, and Graham and Jenny, teenage son and daughter of the manse, were holding a heated discussion, which was nothing unusual.

"Yes, but, Graham, that's the point," Jenny was saying vigorously; "huge families like that are definitely *out* now. It just isn't decent. Dad, you shouldn't take those new people up; your flock will think you are condoning big families, and you know you aren't supposed to do that. It's people like them that take more than a fair share of food and housing and—and schooling and places at university and medical services, and all that. Pass the spuds, Graham, please."

Jenifer's father looked at his daughter with an amused smile.

"You really do seem to be absorbing a little knowledge at last, Jen," he said affectionately. "What a pity it had to wait to be your modern studies. No, Jenny, I'm serious. If you take these big social problems seriously, as I hope and pray you both will, you must also study history and get your facts in proper context. Also you must study human nature and things like motive and purpose as well as emotions. Above all, take trouble to get your facts right before you denounce or proclaim."

"But, Dad, the facts shriek at you: seven children equals—say fourteen grandchildren and at least twenty-eight great-grandchildren."

"Hold it, Jenny! I only said get your facts right.

Your simple arithmetic may be fautless but if you must *judge*, be careful. You may as well know about the Bairds, for I guess we may see quite a lot of them— I certainly hope we shall. You are old enough to understand and keep a confidence, aren't you?"

The two young people nodded. It was just a fact of manse life that one often heard and saw more than one ever passed on outside the walls of home.

"Well, two of the Baird children are their own; the other five have been adopted at various times. So I think on this occasion your objection is over-ruled."

"I guess the two eldest are their own, aren't they? They're awfully alike. Fancy being bothered with all those young ones when they're not your own brothers and sisters. What's the matter with the litte girl in the chair?"

Jenifer was able to switch from one point to another with alacrity and quite able to dismiss her false judgments with a change of slant on the subject under discussion.

"Mary is a spastic, but without serious brain damage. She's everyone's treasure, I gather, without being spoilt. As a matter of fact, Jen, you have jumped to the wrong conclusion, but I'm not telling you which is which. Do you know that the Baird's own two have specially requested their parents that no one here shall know who's who in the family. Do you know why?"

"No, Dad."

"They don't want people to make any distinction in their favour. They want people to treat all the family alike as brothers and sisters. After all, they all bare the same name and are fully adopted and that makes them one family."

Mrs Thompson came back to the immediate moment and asked if anyone wanted any more fruit and custard.

Promptly at four o'clock the door-bell rang, and as soon as the door was opened the hall of the manse seemed to be full of people. Mr Baird introduced the family one by one: Colin and Sue, then Tony and Peter, Mary in her chair, and young Nicholas and Ann. Graham and Jenifer were nowhere to be seen but as they all trooped into the dining-room for tea the two appeared and took their share of entertaining the guests.

It was during the conversation over the tea table that the family's enthusiasm for music came up. At once Mr Thompson was excited. He, too, was a born musician, but the gift had somehow not been passed on to his own two children and in the full life of ministry it had been crowded out. After tea it was a short step to the old little used piano in the corner of the living-room. Sue and Mrs Baird had persuaded Mrs Thompson to let them help her and Jenny clear away, and by the time they came through to join the others the manse was ringing with hymns and choruses.

Graham and Jenifer usually made excuses about the evening services—they had homework to do, exams to work for. But tonight it was different. When they discovered that Colin and Sue and Tony were going with their father, they decided to go, too. Peter took his place at Mary's chair, proud of his responsibility as he walked home with his mother and the two younger children.

"Mum, this is going to be the superest, specialist place to live in. Mr Thompson says the high school is just great: they've won the football shield four years running, *and* been the first in the music festival twice. Primary school is good, too, for music but I'll need to wait for high school for real football."

Mrs Baird smiled down at her young escort. If Peter could find boys to play football with and a school that cared about music, he would be as happy as the proverbial sandboy. Mrs Baird was still smiling at some remark one of the children made as she came level with the corner bungalow. She happened to look up, half aware that someone was watching them. This time Mrs Cooper was caught too late to drop the curtain. Their eyes met, and both smiled, and Mrs Baird gave a friendly wave.

Inexplicably happy, Mrs Cooper waved back and watched them on up the road and out of sight round the corner behind the big trees. The new people, whoever they were, were at least different. They looked interesting, and very responsible.

The Bairds settled down quickly and the people of Middlebridge soon grew accustomed to the sight of Colin, Sue and Tony cycling off to the high school, followed some ten minutes later by Peter, Nicholas and Ann on foot on their way to the primary school near the church. They grew accustomed to seeing the young people with their various musical instruments as well as their school-bags, and they soon came to accept the little girl in the wheelchair as one of themselves and not as something unusual to be stared at or, for some, embarrassed by and turned from. The rumours died down and the family were accepted. Perhaps to many they did seem a little odd, but the charge of being eccentric or even worse was never pursued. To the curious and the more casual they were simply a happy, friendly and rather attractive family; something a little different in a day of so much mass production in the ways of men and affairs.

CHAPTER THREE

THE MYSTERIOUS MR BRIGGS

"Colin, can you spare a moment?" Sue looked up from her homework, a puzzled frown on her face.

"Sure. What's the trouble?"

"This—for Briggs."

"Phew! He's a bit of a character, isn't he?"

Sue nodded. "Do you find him difficult, too?"

"Um. Can't think why, either. I did a perfect bit of transposition for him yesterday when we were getting all those part songs into order, and he said he supposed I had copied it from the original."

"Oh no, Colin!"

"I know. It made me mad for a minute, but I didn't let him see."

"That's about my problem, too. He gets so sarcastic and pitches into me. When I said I'd already done this grade of theory, and sat the exam last year, he just drawled, 'in-cer-red-ible!' just like that, and set me this to do. I think he's copied it out wrongly, because I had this in last year's paper. Look, you can't possibly bar this passage for twelve–eight time—it just won't go. I don't know what to do. I'm not sure if he really doesn't know his stuff or if he's trying to trip me up in front of the class."

"Show me."

Colin reached over and took the theory exercise book from Sue. Mr Briggs had set her a piece to work on on her own as she was ahead of the class, and, as Sue said, it was not correct and couldn't be worked out.

"He's certainly got it wrong."

"Well, what do I do? If I am to get the right answer

I'll have to correct him first and that'll make him mad at me. Look, it's the same here where he has given me this passage for interpretation: he asks me to explain signs and things that don't even come into it."

Colin sat down on the edge of the table, swinging his long legs and thinking the problem over.

"Know what, Sue?"

"No."

"I guess you've rattled him—by accident. I've a hunch you've gone ahead of him. We are the first two to take music for a career for ages—probably since his time—and the others are just time-filling on their programme and taking a rest from their heavier subjects. We're serious, and he'd do this to me probably, only I've already done all my grades that I need in theory. I figure you've over-shot him, and he's bluffing."

Sue shrugged her shoulders.

"That's just too bad for him, isn't it? But what do I do? I've got exams to sit and he's just muddling me up now."

"O.K. Keep calm! I should work it out correctly. In that way you won't confuse yourself, and you are not being horrid and taking him up publicly on it. Leave his alone and put down what you know is right. If he is mad at you at least you know you are blameless, so try and take it and keep your mouth shut. If you must be a musical genius I suppose you'll have to pay the price sooner or later!"

"Musical genius, my foot! Talk sense, Colin! Have you finished your homework?"

"Just on. Why?"

"I'll not be long doing this, and then, if you can rustle up Tony, I'll play the accompaniment for your concerto and maybe we'll have time to look at the new trio."

"It's a good thing we have Hunter and not Briggs

for all our instrumental music. Briggs would paralyse me into playing all the wrong notes."

"Me, too!"

There was silence while Sue finished the work that had caused all the trouble, and then the young people went off to the music room.

"Wouldn't it be grand if we could get a few more folk interested? This could do with an oboe and a viola to really fill it out properly." Sue was glancing over the Haydn Concerto in G which they had recently acquired. Both Sue and Colin were specially gifted, and Tony worked hard with very good results, so that already it was taking shape, and every time they came together they were able to iron out a passage here and a tricky bit of fingering there. Colin was playing the flute, and Tony the violin, while Sue played the piano.

An hour passed and the earlier troubles were more or less forgotten. As the three players sat back and relaxed after their effort they noticed Peter, curled up in the big armchair. Peter was an odd little chap. He was eleven with freckles and the most penetratingly clear blue eyes. His great desire music-wise was to play a trumpet and he had often threatened to run away and join the Salvation Army if no one else would help him. Meantime he was seldom far away when the older children were playing, and his own simple contribution on the violin was really promising. Mr Baird watched and listened to all his family, for apart from 'Kitten' who was everyone's favourite he had no preferences and was always careful to give each one the fullest share of his time and affection.

As Colin was trying over a passage on his flute while Sue counted the beats for him, the phone rang discordantly through the house. Six people flew to answer it.

"I *bags* answer it!" yelled Ann.

"*I* bags, and it's my turn!"

Nicholas had been upstairs and he bounded down so fast that he tripped and sprawled across the hall, adding a shriek to the confusion.

"Be quiet, the lot of you!" Colin admonished them in his most grown-up voice, and he snatched up the receiver. "Yes, Middlebridge 653. Would you mind holding on just a minute, please." He covered the mouthpiece with his hand. "Scram, and stop making such a din. I can't hear a thing."

Sue ushered the two youngest into the kitchen and shut the door firmly and left them protesting and squabbling, while their mother tried once more to check them from the 'bags I' language and habit which she so detested.

Answering the phone was a new delight for the younger members of the family. In the old house it had stood in splendid isolation on the desk in their father's study and they very seldom were near it. Here at Beechwood it was most inconveniently situated in the hall and it had become the latest craze to get to it first and take the call.

With peace restored, Colin carried on the conversation.

"Yes, speaking. Oh yes, sir. Sure, that would be fine ... No, it would be quite all right; they would like it ... Yes, do. Thanks awfully, sir ... Yes, I'll tell Dad."

The boy replaced the receiver.

"Mum! Dad! Where are you?"

Mr and Mrs Baird came at his call and the others were not far away

"That was Mr Hunter, from school, you know. He wants to come and see us, to chat over an idea he's got for reviving the school Music Club."

"Music Club? I didn't know there was one," Sue said.

"There has been, but there isn't, if you get me.

That is just Hunter's point. There used to be a first-class one but people lost interest and he's keen to get it going. He thought if we three were going to join it would give it the boost it needs. Seems everyone is waiting for someone else to move first. He wants to talk it over with us and asked if he could come. That's O.K., isn't it, Mum?"

"Of course, dear. When does he want to come?"

Colin looked at his mother ruefully.

"Well, actually tonight. In about half-an-hour!"

"Colin!"

"But you don't mind, Mum? Not really?"

Mrs Baird laughed.

"You know I don't. But all the same we must get moving and tidy up a bit. Boys, get the room straight and put all those books away; and Sue, come and help cut some extra sandwiches. Fortunately I'd just put ours ready for later on, so all we need do is make a few more."

That was one of the nice things about the Baird home. Everyone was welcome, stray cats and lost dogs and all, and Mrs Baird just calmly laid an extra place, cut a few more sandwiches, or opened another tin as the occasion demanded without ruffling a feather. Beechwood was home and she and her husband were only too thankful that the young people were content to spend so much time in it and to bring their friends home with them. Mrs Baird had the quality of graciousness that kept her at ease with any and everyone, and Mr Baird kept a watching brief over the guests to see that plates were filled, cups replenished and no one was left out on a limb in any conversation.

To say that Mr Hunter enjoyed his visit would be an understatement. Before the younger children were whisked off to bed, at his request the whole family played their own arrangement of a selection of Scots songs. As the three younger children said 'goodnight' and went off with their mother. Mr Hunter turned to Mr Baird.

"This is just about what I've been waiting for. What a pity they aren't all at the High school at the same time! We really could get some club started in that case."

Mr Baird smiled his wise smile and shook his head.

"Too many Bairds could be as bad as too many cooks all in the same place at the same time."

"Have you no special instrument of your own yet, Peter?" Mr Hunter asked as he watched the boy tidy away the music. He had already watched him as he turned over deftly for Colin, who had the heaviest part, with unobtrusive accuracy. "You made a good job of turning over; that means you can read and concentrate —two good qualities for success, Peter."

The boy glowed with pleasure. He was used to doing all the odd jobs and enjoyed being the 'props' man, but it was nice to hear his effort praised.

"I really want to learn to play the trumpet, sir. Or I wouldn't mind the timps," he added modestly.

Mr Hunter hid a smile.

"You do, do you? When do you come to high school?"

"After the summer holidays."

"Well, Peter, if you come to high school I may not be able to produce a trumpet but I will make a drummer of you, and teach you myself if your father's willing."

"Really! Oh, super!"

Peter was away out of the room.

"Mum! Mum! Where are you? Listen to this! Mr. Hunter'll teach me to play the drums at high school."

The young eager voice echoed through the house and the five sitting together in the music room smiled.

"Now, let's get down to business."

Mr Hunter outlined the club as it had been in the past and as he hoped to make it in the near future. Soon Sue and Colin and Tony were throwing in useful suggestions and Mr Baird was sitting back putting in an additional proposal here and there.

"Who *is* really interested?" Sue asked in a lull in the discussion.

Mr Hunter felt in his pocket and brought out a folded sheet of paper.

"For a start there are three Bairds, and with young Peter so near to coming to the high school I'm almost sure we could get him in, especially if you will let me have him as a pupil."

"It's very kind of you. Peter will be delighted and very proud if he is allowed to come. He's a careful boy. He'll fill the house with all the noises of joy when he hears, but it won't go to his head."

"I gather that. Well, there's Joyce Finlay; she used to be very keen: plays the violin and only stopped when she sat her 'O' levels. Paul Ingram is good, too; he plays the oboe, or did, until Joyce dropped out. Then there are about half-a-dozen semi-good, semi-keen players of this and that, strings mostly, but I'm sure they would soon get keen again if only we could make a start. I'll be there to help, of course, and Mrs Dawson —she teaches piano—she will do all she can. Her strong point is encouraging young players and making them see what they can achieve."

"And Mr Briggs?"

Sue asked the question slowly and deliberately. She just *had* to know. Mr Hunter looked up sharply and his tone was sharp when he answered.

"We'll leave Mr Briggs out of this—not his line at all."

And with that he changed the subject.

Two days later a notice went up on the board at school to the effect that there would be a meeting of the revived Music Club, and all interested should speak to Mr Hunter and attend on Friday at 4.15 p.m. in the large music room.

It was also two days later that Sue had her first real brush with Mr Briggs. She had handed in her homework along with the rest of the class. Following Colin's advice she had done the work correctly without drawing any attention to Mr Brigg's errors. The result was disastrous. Mr Briggs returned the corrected exercises for all the class except Sue.

"Study your work and note my corrections carefully," he said in a sharp little staccato voice. "That's the way to learn what not to do next time."

Sue thought, He's playing for time, remembering Colin's hunch. She drew a deep breath and then raised her hand. At first the master appeared not to notice, then he turned slowly towards her.

"Yes?"

"Please, sir, my work hasn't been returned."

"Is that so? And did you submit work for me to correct?"

In her agitation Sue missed the point of his chosen words. She should have remembered that there was probably nothing in her work to be corrected. But she was taking the phrase in its more general sense.

"Yes, sir, I did."

Mr Briggs shuffled through some papers on his desk. Then he held out a few sheets for Sue to see.

"Do you mean this?" he asked.

"Yes, sir."

Carefully and with precision Mr Briggs tore the sheets across and across and dropped them in the waste-paper basket.

"I'm not accustomed to teaching children who adjust

the set questions to suit their limitation of musical knowledge, and I do not mark original work. This is a theory class, not composition."

An uncomfortable titter ran round the room. Sue flushed and bit back the words on her lips.

That was only the beginning. For the next three lessons Mr Briggs either ignored Sue and her work or found some excuse for denouncing it. At first the others in the class were puzzled and then indignant of his treatment of Sue, but when they found that she refused to take issue with him they shrugged their shoulders and lost interest.

By now the Music Club was active again and Sue threw herself wholeheartedly into supporting it. Mr Hunter was delighted with the response. Seventeen young musicians of varying talent with a variety of instruments had joined. The main weekly meeting took place in the school but there were smaller groups meeting for practice from time to time, usually in the Baird home. It seemed to Sue that the more the club flourished the more bitterly Mr Briggs attacked her. Apart from the unpleasantness and the injustice of it, Sue was getting worried. In a matter of weeks she had exams to sit, and not only was she not getting the teaching she needed but all the trouble was making her confused so that she was in doubt at times what was wrong and what was right. She toyed with the idea of speaking to Mr Hunter and dismissed it at once. It would put him into a very difficult position.

At last she could stand it no longer and one evening she went in search of her father.

"Busy, Dad?" she asked, knowing well what answer she would get.

"Always busy, thank God," he said simply, "but never too busy to listen. What's troubling you these days, lass?"

Sue smiled to herself. She might have known that she had not managed to hide her problem from her parents, no matter how hard she tried.

She told the tale, ungarnished with any unnecessary details.

"Colin has a hunch that Mr Briggs is a bit at sea," she finished. "He thinks perhaps I've passed him, but I wish he'd do something else about it instead of just muddling me up."

John Baird sat silently considering the story. He never came to impulsive conclusions. He weighed things up carefully and tried to see the other point of view whenever possible.

"When is your next theory lesson?" he asked.

"Wednesday."

"And this is Friday. Leave it with me, Sue, and stop worrying. There will be a way through. All right?"

"Yes thanks, Dad."

Sue turned to go.

"How's the club shaping now?"

She came back and perched on the arm of her father's chair.

"Oh, super, Dad! Isn't it strange—the evening that Mr Hunter came round to talk about it, Colin and Tony and I had just been wishing we had more to play that Hadyn Concerto—and here we are now hard at it with all we need. It's gorgeous fun, too, playing together like this, and most of the members are really dead keen."

"And who, may I ask, is the little bit of fluff that comes along and would like you to think she was one of the great masters herself when she plays!"

"Oh, Deidre! Isn't she a scream? She is so *very* full of 'soul' and she sits and drools over the piano and doesn't impress anyone except with annoyance. Some doting relative has told her how brilliant she is and she's believed them, poor kid! Most of the crowd tolerate her and a few can't stand her."

"And you? What's your reaction to m'lady?"

Sue laughed.

"I rather like her, Dad. She is so transparently hopeless yet awhile, and will be until she stops thinking she's wonderful and has nothing to learn. But she is a generous soul and has a heart of gold when she isn't acting and making a fool of herself. And she can be great fun, too, when she forgets to be dramatic."

Mr Baird eyed Sue with interest. She always had this gift of seeing people apart from their blatant faults and finding something likeable in their make-up.

"Try to forget this man Briggs for a bit, Sue, as far as this trouble is concerned. You know there is a pernicious evil known as 'professional jealousy'. It is a deadly poison and why he should suffer from it on your account I don't know; but if this is the cause, then he is to be pitied rather than feared. Now, go to Colin. He has piped that first flute phrase to you three times over like the wise thrush. If I'm not much mistaken, that is his way of calling you to his aid."

Sue went happily. When Dad took things over they had a way of working out.

CHAPTER FOUR

THE CRITICS

Mr Briggs, whatever his reason, was not the only adverse critic of the Baird family and their invasion of Middlebridge. Jenifer Thompson came in one evening ready to unload her moans on to anyone who would listen.

"That Baird crowd!" she exploded, banging down her schoolbag with unnecessary force. "They need to be taught a thing or two, and the sooner the better!"

"Hey, there, Jen!" Graham looked up from a plate of pie and chips. "What's bitten you?"

"Gently please, Jenny. It's not like you to speak like that. What's the trouble?"

Mrs Thompson set down her daughter's plate in her place and then poured her a cup of tea.

"Thanks, Mum. Well, it's just about everything. Because *they've* come, old Hunter has revived the Music Club and lots of silly sheep have gone flocking into it— goodness knows why. I'm sure half of them don't know a fiddle from a trombone."

"Sour grapes!" muttered her inelegant brother, helping himself to a large slice of home-baked fruit cake.

"Graham, please!"

Mr Thompson seldom interfered in the lively tea-time conversation that was largely in the hands of the two young people but he did insist on courtesy. Both children knew it, and usually kept the unwritten rules carefully. Whenever Mr Thompson was confronted with the old saying, 'Boys will be boys', he was quick to retort that that might be so, but it did not prevent learning to be well-bred young men.

"What have those dreadful Bairds done to annoy you, Jenny?" he asked, lightening the atmosphere with his tone and his twinkle.

"It's about the same everywhere, Dad. Joan says the Guides are losing members because some of the girls have joined the club, and Ron Paterson says the same is happening in the parish church youth club. Half the kids are switching over to music groups on their own. I don't think it's fair."

"Jen's right, Dad. The B.B. and the Scouts are muttering the same complaints. Middlebridge is going music daft for no reason at all. Only four turned up to the Debating Society last night, too."

"Ho! Ho! That's a good one," Jen turned the tables on her brother. "How many usually go? Six, and you are one of last night's absentees—very funny!"

Jenifer paused long enough to make an unladylike grimace at her brother, finished her chips and started on again about the same subject.

"Honestly, Dad, it's like having 'The Sound of Music' dropped in on you for breakfast, dinner, tea and supper, having those Bairds around now."

"How you do exaggerate, Jenny," her mother said. "Pass your father's cup and get on with your tea. Remember, I've got a committee meeting here tonight and your father is out, so you can take your lessons into the study."

Both Mr and Mrs Thompson were to hear more of this feeling concerning the Bairds as they went about their work over the next few weeks. Mr Thompson spent a good deal of time and thought sifting over the comments and criticisms. Then he went to see Miss Craig, an elderly, almost housebound member of his congregation. In spite of her age and physical limitations she could usually be relied on to see further round corners than most, and to come up with some solution worthy of consideration.

Over a cup of tea and some of her excellent short-bread the minister outlined the problem. It did not affect him and his organisations, because the new-comers were members of his congregation and he had gained, rather than lost, through their arrival. But he could see how others might be feeling—how he might be feeling if the Bairds had thrown in their lot with one of the other congregations and it was his work that was getting the draught.

Miss Craig refilled the minister's teacup and slid another piece of shortbread on to his plate while he was not looking.

"This interests me very much," she said. "As a matter of fact, I had Tom Hunter here last night. I've not met the Bairds yet to speak to, but I must say I like the look of them and all I've heard about them. Tom came with a different kind of problem. The eldest girl, Sue, has fallen into trouble with the caustic tongue of Billy Briggs, and only you and I know what that will mean. However, the girl has to sit a theory exam soon and he is wrecking her chances. I could speak to Bill but I don't think he is ready for that yet. Instead, I've said I'll take the girl for a few lessons and get her brushed up. She can sit out his lessons and save his face. I gather she is the kind that will do that, and her father is the same. I like that type. They can stand on their feet and fight righteous battles, usually for the sake of others, but they don't go about stirring up mud just for the sake of being fussily important. But now, about your own problem; when is the next big united effort in Middlebridge?"

"United? Oh, I see! There's the big youth rally at end of June; you know, the end of all the organisations for the summer and the closing rally of the C.E. Is that what you mean?"

"Capital! Especially as the Christian Endeavour are in charge of the evening session. Can't you get this band, or choir, or—no, it's a group, nowadays, isn't it?"

Mr Thompson laughed. Typical of Miss Craig, who was over eighty, to be in tune with the current jargon.

"Yes, by saying 'group' you are definitely up-to-date."

Miss Craig laughed, too. These two were on the same wave-length in most things and understood each other perfectly.

"Well, get this group organised into that day. I'm sure they will see for themselves, without needing it to be pointed out, that each organisation is of value and that each needs the loyalty of its members. I don't think people like these Bairds need to be pushed hard before they get their priorities right; after all, they've only been here about two months and already they have been drawn into some pretty heavy commitments. I doubt if they've had time to look round and see what else is going on here, yet."

"Right, as usual, I guess! I'll work something out and then get around the others responsible for the rally and see what we can do. After all, the music at the rallies the last few years has been pathetic. I could have wept for Tom last year; he worked so hard, and so many people let him down at the last moment. I suppose it is hardly surprising that he has jumped at new talent when it has been put right at his feet."

Mr Thompson worked carefully and made a well-thought-out plan before he approached his brother ministers in the town and the leaders of the various organisations who would share the rally. First he showed it to Tom Hunter, who was enthusiastic. That made two of them, and even Graham and Jenifer saw the wisdom in the idea and promised to do what they could to make it a success. The disgruntled leaders were less optimistic; but as the scheme got around, the chilly atmosphere grew a little warmer. There was certainly room for improvement in the musical side of the day's events, and something could be said for even hymns and marches being well-played instead of blundered through any old way.

Sue laughed when she heard some of the comments that were being made.

"Dad, isn't it odd, the tone in which some people say 'even hymn-tunes'. It sounds as if hymns were beneath the notice of real musicians. I guess Wesley would turn in his grave if he heard it! "

"Is Wesley in his grave, Sue?" Ann asked. She had crept into the room unnoticed by her elders. "I would have expected Wesley to be with Jesus in heaven if he's dead. Is he?"

"Little pitchers! " muttered Mr Baird under his breath. "Talk yourself out of that one if you can, Sue! " He twinkled at her.

Sue drew the little girl to her.

"Yes, Ann, you are quite right. Wesley isn't really in a grave—that's just a silly, thoughtless thing that silly, thoughtless grown-ups say."

"You're not silly and thoughtless, Sue. Why do grown-ups say it?" Ann skipped from one thought to the next.

"All they mean—or at least, all *I* meant—was that Wesley thought hymns were gloriously worth giving super tunes to, and he would never have understood people who made out that any old tune would do, sung and played in any old way."

Tony had wandered over, curious to hear Sue extricate herself, and he grinned at his father as they both listened with mutual understanding.

"Not a bad wriggle out, eh, Dad? But Sue is right. I told Mr Johnson at school that I wanted to learn to play the organ so that I could play for the services and, just as Sue says, he said: 'Oh, hymns! anyone can play those!' It is odd, isn't it, Dad?"

Mr Baird nodded in agreement.

"I must say I really do enjoy a well-tuned Salvation Army band for that very reason." Mrs Baird came in in time to hear the drift of the conversation, and to join in. "It is so robust and it makes the old hymns sound like the songs of people who meant business and could be strong to stand firm, and be a happy people at one and the same time."

"That's how I like to hear them," Sue said, quietly; "even more so when I hear a hymn being sung in unison with a piano, or even an organ, if it sounds poverty-stricken, as is so often the case. In my head I can hear all the gorgeous chords and harmonies that would be so exciting if we had a choir and a band and an orchestra all at once to help us."

"Sure you don't want all the heavenly choir to join it, too, Sue?" her father teased gently. "I know what you mean, though. Maybe one day we will make music like that to the glory of God in our churches. Meanwhile you have Sir Arthur to encourage you as you wait to hear your own 'lost chords'. You will hear them one day just as surely as he has by now."

"It'll be some day when I do!"

CHAPTER FIVE

SUE MEETS MISS CRAIG

Before the rally was due, two special events occupied the Bairds. The first was Tony's fifteenth birthday, and he got everything he wanted, or so he said. Sue and Colin pooled their resources and gave him an L.P. of three of the Bach Brandenburg Concertos, Peter and Mary gave him a coveted paperback 'thriller' by his favourite author, Nicholas and Ann had worked together and made him a notebook that would fit in his violin case, with every other page ruled—a little wobbly, perhaps—in stave ruling; to make it more useful still they had attached a pencil to a cord which was knotted on to the back of the book and, as a further bonus, had a small piece of indiarubber on the end of it. Various aunts and uncles sent him postal orders, but his most treasured present came from the parents and all four grandparents—a really good violin to replace the under-sized, rather battered instrument on which he had learned since he was seven years old. His pleasure had to be witnessed for he had no words left to say anything. His face was pink with excitement and he stood fingering it gently, opening and shutting his mouth in an effort to say 'thank-you', his eyes bright and complete surprise written all over his face.

"Bags I have his old one!" Nicholas burst out.

The spell of that first long moment of intense pleasure was broken, but Tony was hardly aware of his young brother's intrusion. He was already tuning his new treasure and softly trying out its tone.

"Mum, can I?" Nicholas insisted.

Mrs Baird looked at the small bundle of persistence. Ann was already gingerly, hopefully laying a little possessive hand on the old fiddle and at Nicholas' demands the corners of her mouth had drooped.

"You know what I think about children who use that horrid expression, Nicky. It's Dad's old fiddle, anyway, and it's for him to say what happens to it. Personally I think you should both share it, you and Ann, until we see how you are both shaping. But you must do your other practice first and your schoolwork, just as the older ones did before they started a second instrument. And remember, Nicky, it is 'ladies first'."

"That's right, Mummy," Mr Baird joined in.

"And what about Peter?" Ann asked. Peter and his interests were never far from Ann's thoughts.

'I don't think Peter is interested, Ann, bless you. He can share it if he is, of course."

"Are you, Pete?" Ann slid her little hand confidingly into his big one.

The boy shook his head.

'No thanks. 'Toot-toot-tootle-toot' for me." He made a fair imitation of a trumpet, of sorts. "That's all I want. Dad, I won't really have to wait till *I'm* fifteen before I get one, will I? That's ages and ages."

"We'll see. You are nearly twelve now, and you've the drums to keep you happy meantime."

"Oh, I know, Dad. But three *years*! It's just not possible—why, I'll be so *old* by then."

Everyone laughed and Mr Baird reminded them that, birthday or no birthday, there was school and time was getting on. Tony found it hard to tear himself away but at last they were all off and Mr and Mrs Baird and Mary were left to tidy up the envelopes and papers, clear the breakfast and lay plans for a birthday tea.

The second event concerned Sue. Unknown to her,

her father had consulted Tom Hunter about her theory problem. What was said between the two men Sue never knew but the outcome was that one day Mr Hunter gave her a letter to take to a Miss Craig for him. Miss Craig, he said, lived a few doors away from the church and was willing to help her with her theory work.

"You'll like Miss Craig," he had said when he handed over the letter. "She's expecting you. This is just a personal note on another matter. She's an old friend of mine, but I thought if you took this instead of me taking it it would help to break the ice. It's a bit difficult standing on a strange doorstep saying, 'I'm Sue Baird', isn't it?"

Sue took the envelope gratefully. Mr Hunter managed to do so many thoughtful things. What a pity Mr Briggs couldn't catch a little of the same spirit. What a pity that anyone had to be so crabby and sarcastic. Life would be so much easier, Sue thought to herself as she walked away, if only people would at least be nice to each other.

Sue cycled home and told her mother about the letter. Mrs Baird nodded.

"Yes, Dad knows about it. Go up and get tidy while I make the tea and then you can go round immediately after and do your homework when you get back."

Upstairs, Sue tidied her hair after changing into a clean blouse. She looked at her shoes and decided they needed a good brushing. Downstairs, she laid out her theory books and sharpened her pencil. A sense of freedom from a nagging worry possessed her and she went happily in to tea.

What she had expected she did not know, but it was certainly not what she found. In answer to her ring at the bell of the trim little bungalow there was a

pause and then the sound of a distant door shutting.
Sue stood looking at the neat garden in front of the
house and when the door suddenly opened she was
unprepared for the sight of a little old lady, nearly
bent double and with a short stick in either hand.

"I'm looking for Miss Craig."

"And I am Miss Craig, and you will be Sue Baird.
Come in, my dear. Go straight on into the room on
your right. It takes me a little time. Old bones
demand respect and I have learnt to humour them a
little."

Talking easily, Miss Craig followed the girl into the
pleasant room. A table was drawn up in front of the
fireplace, and books and papers were spread out ready
for work to begin.

"Mr Hunter asked me to give you this," Sue said,
handing over the letter as they both sat down.

"Thank you, Sue. Mr Hunter is one of my very good
friends, and his letters between his visits do a lot to
keep me cheery."

Sue noticed that there was a lovely Newfoundland
dog stretched out on the hearthrug close to Miss
Craig's chair. He was growling softly at her.

Miss Craig patted his massive shoulder.

"It's all right, Honey. We're all friends here."

"What a lovely name for a dog—'Honey'!" Sue
exclaimed.

The dog, hearing her name, raised her head majes-
tically and gazed at Sue.

"Lie down! Good dog!" commanded her mistress,
and Honey lay back contented with her small world.

After a few preliminary questions the lesson began
in earnest. Miss Craig was a born teacher and Sue's
problems were rapidly disappearing. Her spirits rose
as she realised that, at this rate, she would soon catch
up the time she had lost with Mr Briggs.

It was during her third lesson that she came to understand a little more about Miss Craig herself. She had seen at once that she was badly crippled, and had instantly admired her courage so evident in the way she lived alone and managed to do most things for herself. But it was while Sue was struggling wearily with a difficult passage which she could not seem to harmonise that she saw her new friend in a fresh light. Sue was making the most elementary mistakes and was annoyed with herself, expecting every minute that Miss Craig would justly lose patience with her. Instead, the old lady watched her in silence for a few minutes, then she leant over and gently closed Sue's books and took the hot and sticky pencil out of her hand.

"Have you had a busy day?" she asked, her tone kindly.

Sue nodded. Tears of disappointment were not far away and she bit hard to keep them back.

"Sit back and relax. One of the lessons I've learnt with old age is to stop rushing in with the proverbial fools, and side with the slower angels instead! It helps in all sorts of things, not only in minding one's business. It conserves energy for the more important affairs, and things have a way of looking different viewed from a distance."

Sue obediently sat back. Relaxing was another matter. She felt knotted up all over with her efforts. She heard Miss Craig get up out of her chair but she did not look up. She was blindly studying the pattern on the carpet in a frantic attempt to regain her self-control. And then, softly, from across the room came the notes of the piano. Sue looked up then quickly, amazed to see the little bent figure perched on the edge of the piano stool, her gnarled old fingers making music for Sue's comfort. Sue swallowed back her tears desperately and found she could relax after all. The music rose and fell softly. It seemed fantastic that so much power could come through so frail and pained a body, but it did. For fully fifteen minutes Miss Craig played on and then, slowly, she came back and stood, one hand on Sue's shoulder. She looked down with her calm, unclouded smile into the girl's face.

"Better?"

"Oh yes, much better, thanks. I was just silly. I couldn't seem to think even the most ordinary, simple things. I've had two exams today and I've two more tomorrow, and I suppose I just let them get on top of me."

"We all do, at your age, my dear. That is when all the pressures are piled on us and we are not fully matured to bear them. It is only when we are too old to be taking exams that we learn how to be wise in the use of our time and our energies."

They talked on quietly for a few minutes and then Miss Craig told Sue to pack up her books and come back when her other exams were all behind her.

Sue walked out to her cycle and rode home with her mind full of what she had seen and heard. She had guessed that Miss Craig was more than a teacher of theory but she had never dreamt that she was such a fine pianist, far less that she would still be able to play.

Tom Hunter explained the miracle to Sue. Miss Craig had been a brilliant pianist in her earlier years but had been crippled as a result of a car accident. After that, arthritis had overtaken her, or as she preferred to say 'caught up' with her but never quite overtaken her. Day after day through the years she had schooled herself little by little to make her fingers obey her, and now that little was one of her rare pleasures. In her small world where friends were always welcome, she still had many hours to pass alone, and the self-discipline of those early years now stood by her faithfully. Her calm faith had taken hold of her misfortunes and minted them into a currency that bought many hours of peace for herself and left her plenty to share with those who knew her best.

"She's rather special," Mr Hunter summed up simply and a little proudly when Sue had shyly asked him about his friend.

Sue agreed.

"You know, Sue, she is eighty-six, but don't you dare let on I've told you!"

Eighty-six and still full of such a spirit! Sue marvelled as she went back to her own classroom from her chat in the music room with Mr Hunter. Whatever would she be like at that age—with or without those handicaps? She remembered Mr Thompson saying once in a sermon that too many people regarded old age as a time to sow all the things in their lives they had never given time to earlier, but that in fact it was a time when other people would reap the harvest, good or bad, of what one had sown for oneself all through life. People like Miss Craig proved his point.

Sue sat her theory exam in June and went over the paper afterwards with Miss Craig, and they both thought she had done quite well. The long summer days were on them and for Sue they were seldom long enough for the swimming events and the tennis matches, the athletics and all the extra rehearsals for the school end-of-term concert and the coming youth rally.

CHAPTER SIX

A COMMITTEE MEETING

"Dad, they want a committee to serve for the final arrangements for the rally, and they want you to be chairman. You will, won't you?"

Colin poked his head round the study door and surprised Mr Baird with the question.

"Me? Oh, no, Colin! That would be sticking my neck out, when we've so newly come. It's different for you folk who are all playing, but not me, not on a committee level. Ask Mr Thompson or Mr Hunter."

"Nothing doing, Dad. They're both on it and it wouldn't do for them to chair it. They want someone 'impartial and good-tempered'—that's you, Dad! We had hoped to get Miss Craig, actually, but I suppose it is asking too much and it was she who nominated you, and the others all fell for the suggestion."

Mr Baird pushed back his chair and came round and sat on the front of his desk facing Colin.

"So, I am not to try and wriggle out, is that it?"

"Not really, Dad. Do take it; you really are the right one for it. You see, there are still a few tricky points to iron out, and everyone knows everyone else too well and you've no axe to grind and you really will do it beautifully!"

"And since when have you learnt to be a young charmer, eh? All right, I'll have a shot at it if that's the way it's got to be."

The first meeting was held on the following evening

and it moved slowly through the agenda. Everyone was being diplomatic and a little cautious. The date was already fixed but the timing had to be gone into more exactly and the programme co-ordinated and various innovations discussed. It was when the programme was under discussion that the sparks began to fly. Naturally enough each man present wanted his own organisation given prominence.

The early items were fairly easily disposed of. All taking part were to meet at the farthest point and march with the bands playing to the town hall for the display and rally. So far so good. Suggestions were being thrown backwards and forwards across the table and extra items being squeezed in to keep the peace with a leader here or an officer there. Colin was sitting quietly; he and Sue were representing the Music Club. Colin was busy, apparently doing sums on the back of an old envelope. In a pause when the chairman asked if anyone had anything else to say, Colin got up.

"Mr Chairman, I've been roughly working out the time of this suggested programme and I think we are forgetting how long it will take. At the rate we are going we'll be there till midnight!"

There was a mild rustling of papers and scraping of chairs. A round-faced, genial man whose name Colin did not know tapped the table impatiently with his pencil.

"And why not? The kids around here don't get all that much excitement. Give 'em a night out for once, boy; they can always sleep it off next morning. We went home with the milk once in a while when I was a lad!"

"I don't want to spoil anyone's fun," Colin faced the man frankly. "But it is Saturday night, not Friday, that we are talking about."

"So what? All the more time to sleep in on Sunday."

Colin flushed, but held his ground.

"Not everyone will want to do that, sir," he said quietly. "I for one want to go to church and, well—I don't think it is quite courteous to our ministers to stick up half the night and be all in on Sunday morning."

More papers rustled, more chairs scraped. The men of the committee were watching Colin closely. Mr Thompson and Mr Baird caught each others' glances but neither was in a position to take up the matter at the moment. There was silence. Then Mr Hunter got to his feet—casually, almost languidly, giving little idea of how he felt personally.

"The boy has got a point. If he can frame it into a reasonable proposal I'll second it. His argument seems to make sense."

Sue hastily passed a scribbled note to her brother. Colin scanned it unobtrusively and got to his feet again.

"Thank you, Mr Hunter. I propose that in view of the extended programme this year the rally starts at two-thirty instead of four-thirty. That should give time for all the items to be enjoyed without a rush."

"I second that." Mr Hunter was on the ball at once.

A pause.

"Those in favour?"

Seven hands were raised at once, two followed a little more slowly, and finally the remaining three made the necessary indication.

"Carried unanimously!"

A few final arrangements were settled and the committee meeting was over. Mr Thompson drove Mr Baird and Colin and Sue home. No reference was made to Colin's part in the meeting and the boy was grateful.

During the final week before the rally Miss Craig asked Sue if she could spare the time to do something for her. She wanted some roses from her garden cut and taken to her niece's grave in the nearby cemetery.

"I used to manage to go myself at one time, but for the past five years I haven't managed it."

"Of course I'll go—I'll be glad to, but——"

"But what, my dear?"

Sue blushed.

"I was only wondering about the five years; surely Mr Hunter would be only to pleased to have taken you. He'd do anything for you, I'm sure."

Miss Craig twinkled.

"Yes, Sue, Tommy would do anything for me, as you say, and he does far more than even your sharp young eyes will ever see, but—well, there are some things you don't ask a man to do for you. This is just a little sentimental journey. It is old and sentimental women who go on putting flowers on the graves of the young 'just because', and we don't ask our gallant men to do it for us. I know Madeline is not there, but the stone is, and I like to think it is not altogether forgotten. You'll find it quite easily; it's the one nearest the path on the far side to your left as you go in the main gate, and it is five rows back. And then, my dear, come back and we'll have tea together. I have strawberries out of the garden!"

Sue rode off on her cycle, the roses strapped to her carrier. As Miss Craig had said it was easy to find, and soon she was standing in front of the stone. Amazed, she read and re-read the words and then swiftly knelt to put the flowers in place. For a long moment she knelt there reading and re-reading the stone. It ran:

In loving memory of
MADELINE CRAIG
beloved wife of
WILLIAM BRIGGS,
tragically killed
June 21st, 1955
aged 34,
also Susan Mary,
aged 12.

Sue pieced it all together as best she could. The accident that robbed Miss Craig of her mobility would have been about then. And Susan would have been Mr Briggs' daughter. No wonder, oh, no wonder! And yet why? Why did these things have to happen, and why did people have to come out of them bitter? There was Mr Briggs, at odds with himself and his world; and there was Miss Craig, at peace with herself and her world. What was it Dad had said about Mr Briggs needing to be pitied rather than feared? As usual Dad was so right.

Back at tea with Miss Craig, Sue found the subject was not to be discussed. Beyond a casual, 'you found the place?' called from the tiny kitchen as Sue entered, Miss Craig kept the conversation on other lines and Sue was aware that she was meant to take her cue from her friend and leave her questions unasked and unanswered. Miss Craig had trusted her, and that was enough. Whatever else was involved, Sue was not meant to probe into it.

CHAPTER SEVEN

THE YOUTH RALLY

The last Saturday in June was dry and sunny and hot. The final combined rehearsal the day before had been about as bad as it could be, so everyone was keyed up on the day itself to produce something much better. Miss Craig's windows looked on to the arrival point for all the marchers as they approached the town hall steps, and she had invited Mrs Baird and Mary to join her there at her grandstand seats. Later, Mr Thompson was coming to fetch them all over to seats of honour in the hall for the programme itself.

Everything went off well, and by six-thirty the audience and young performers settled down to enjoy the last item on the long day's schedule, the closing rally service in the hands of the local branch of the Christian Endeavourers. The Salvation Army band sat in the centre of the orchestra, flanked by the high School orchestra, while the massed choirs sat on the platform. How they all sang! The C.E. had given the choice of three of the hymns to the local O.A.P. group, and the old familiar words and music of 'What a Friend We Have in Jesus', 'Abide With Me', and 'The Church's One Foundation' filled the hall as all the instruments, choirs and the audience joined it. But it was when they were playing Luther's great words and music, 'A Safe Stronghold our God is Still', and the brass and the drums and the strings and the wind instruments were playing as they had never managed to play in the rehearsals, that Sue felt her longings for 'real music' were being satisfied. Boy trebles from the parish church sang a twentieth-century hymn and for two verses were accompanied by the children's own recorder group.

At last the end was in sight and there remained only the united act of dedication. The choirs and the players found their copies of the closing hymn and the hymn-sheets rustled through the hall like wind in the trees as the audience turned over to the last page. Sue played the familiar air automatically. It was a tune she knew by memory and, she thought, by heart. As the verses followed one after another she was aware that the words were penetrating in their depth of meaning. Life, wonderful with opportunity, lay ahead of her. Suddenly she felt insignificant, helpless and the world vast and unmanageable. And God? What was she singing? 'Take . . . take . . . take . . .; my life, my moments and my days, my hands, feet, voice, . . . my all . . .' Did she want anyone else to take them, even God? Most of all, God? Suppose He had plans for her other than her own? Was she prepared to let Him have His way with her? She played on, her playing controlled by long discipline of practice so that it did not betray the chaos of her thoughts. If she were honest, she knew she could not say 'take'; she could only say 'Help me and put my mixed-up values right. I want my own way. If it's not Your way, I'll need Your help more than ever. I know Your way will be best, but I'm not ready for it if it isn't my way.' The hymn came to a triumphant finish and Mr Thompson gave the prayer of dedication and the blessing in a stilled and silent building.

There was a long hush after the magnificently sung and played seven-fold 'Amen', and then quietly, reverently, the movement away from the front began like waves. No one seemed inclined to chatter as instruments were packed away, music collected, coats and bags found. By the time the town hall clock chimed out its ten strokes the hall was empty and in darkness.

Mr Baird, Mr Thompson and Mr Hunter escorted Miss Craig home, and Mr Hunter did the honours for her by producing a cup of tea for their guests.

"Not too tired?" he asked quietly as he handed her a cup.

She smiled up at him with her usual twinkling smile.

"Absolutely exhausted, as you well know, Tom!"

"You'll be all right, though?" his tone showed his anxiety.

"Of course! Go and look after our guests."

As they sat talking, they went over the highlights of the evening.

"A great success!" Miss Craig pronounced it all.

"You think so?" Mr Baird asked. "I'm always so afraid of too many Bairds around."

The little old lady laughed.

"Oh well, you were thoroughly outnumbered to-night so you can sleep with an easy mind. But what does it matter? Your family have so much to give and they give generously and spontaneously. Let others learn to receive and share their gifts. All our young folk can get on together happily that way. I must say I think the experiment worked very well. There was such a warm and friendly atmosphere, and that has been missing in the last few years."

"Strange how participating and sharing music does something to people—I suppose it is some sort of primeval instinct, you know, the tribal camp-fire atmosphere."

"Yes, Tom, I'm sure you are right. I've read, and firmly believe, that 'the family that prays together stays together', and I think those who make music and play together go a long way to solving some of life's most divisive problems. We learn how independent we are."

Later, when Tom Hunter and Miss Craig were alone, she gave a long sigh. Tom looked up sharply.

"You *are* tired out. Can I get you anything? Do anything?"

"No thank you, Tom. Just sit with me for a while. I don't like my own thoughts at the moment. I'm bitterly disappointed."

"Disappointed? You've been saying what a success it was. It's not like you to say one thing and think another."

"It's not that, Tom. I meant what I said to the others; I know it has been a memorable day for Middlebridge. But you see, I sent a personal invitation to Bill, to be my guest and, well—he did not even reply, and I had so hoped today might see a little healing of the breach. Sometimes I begin to think it will not happen in my life-time and when I'm not here Bill will have to bear his most bitter thoughts alone, and I know him well enough to know that one day he will come to himself and feel desolate. I would like to be here then, for if I am gone there will be little he can do about it."

Tom sat and studied his clasped hands. Miss Craig's forebearance with the stubborn, churlish Briggs was about the only matter on which they did not see eye to eye. Tom knew how deeply the man had hurt this frail, gallant old lady and it took him all his time to keep his tongue, and his hands, off the trouble-maker.

"All right, Tom my dear." Miss Craig spoke out of long experience. "I know you cannot understand and I don't expect you to. Bill is a disagreeable contemporary for you, not much good at his job, and outside that I know you try to show him Christian charity and I know you to be sincere. To me, Bill will always be

Maddy's husband and little Susan's adored daddy and, for a while, a great and charming friend to me. My disability embarrasses him as I believe does my forgiveness of him, but I find it increasingly hard to forgive him the mischief he makes for others such as Sue Baird, and yet I must forgive because I myself depend on God's forgiveness and shall need to do so to the very end of the road. I dare not covet what I will not give. Now, Tom, it is late and you must go on your way. You mustn't be 'discourteous to Mr Thompson' and nod in his sermon tomorrow! I love that attitude of Colin's; it is so diplomatic and yet so real to him. What a pity we are not all more 'courteous' to one another these days; it is such a splendid word for such a splendid quality. It reminds me of the old gracious minuets where one instrument seems to be bowing politely to another and the composer did not dare introduce harsh discords to break into the serenity. I try to follow modern music but to my old ears much of it sounds like people being angry with each other. Good-night, Tom. Give my love to Jean and come again soon."

Next evening Sue looked in to see Miss Craig. Now that the theory lessons were over for the time being, she still looked in sometimes and cheered her friend with news of what was going on at school and at home and amongst the young folk at the church.

"Have you met Marie Richardson yet?" Miss Craig asked in a lull in the conversation about the previous day's success.

"No—not to know of, anyway. I've met a lot of new faces that I can't put a name to yet, in these last days."

"You won't have met Marie over the rally; she has been away on some course to do with her work, but I hope you will meet her soon. I think you'll find you have a good deal in common."

Sue made no comment. She was wary of having new friendships made for her. Miss Craig read her thoughts.

"I only mean that you and Marie have many of the same good qualities and, I believe, much the same outlook on life in general. Marie is no 'super' person to be afraid of; she is just rather special to me because I have known her all her life and watched her grow up and make the big decisions life demands of us all. She has all that it takes to be a first-class musician, but by profession she is a welfare advisor in a factory and she often finds herself in the most unharmonious situations. The point is this: she works hard at a very mundane, routine job in order to keep the home going for her step-mother, who is a widow, and her two young step-brothers. In her spare time she runs a music club in the poorer end of the city. Three nights a week she stays late after work—which is one reason why we seldom see her except on Sundays—and she divides the club up so that one night she has the under twelves, the next the twelve to fifteens and a few older ones who are keen to stay on after fifteen, and on the third evening she visits handicapped children in their homes and gives them music, too."

Sue sat and listened with interest. She was beginnig to see that 'doing music' could mean a great deal more than getting to the top, or somewhere near it, and becoming professional. What did she really want out of life? 'Take—take—take. . . .' The words of last night came back into her mind. Did she want to give all she had, all that had first been given to her, back into the safe-keeping of God?

"I would like to meet Marie," she said as she got up to go.

"I expect you will. She was here for lunch today and had been in church this morning. She is very interested in your little Mary, and she was very pleased to hear all about the rally."

That night Sue looked around before the service started and decided that the girl in the blue and white dress, with an older woman and two young boys, must be Marie. She was not surprised when they came out at the end to see this girl speaking to her parents nor to hear them invite her for supper the following Sunday evening.

CHAPTER EIGHT

THE ACCIDENT

It usually took quite a time for all the Baird family to be home together on Sunday evenings. It was a time of leisurely freedom in which friendships were made and cemented. The parents often came home first, leaving the younger members of the family to talk with the other young people in the congregation. More often than not it meant that when they did come home each one brought a friend with them, and Mr and Mrs Baird welcomed them warmly. There was always a good supply of sandwiches and home-baked cakes, always enough to go round, and 'going back to the Bairds' had become a popular way to round off the happy Sundays the young people spent that summer.

A week after Sue's talk with Miss Craig, Marie Richardson walked home with Mr and Mrs Baird. Sue had taken the church flowers to Miss Craig and would be following quickly. In all there were about a dozen young people filling up the living-room when the telephone rang shrilly through the house above all the noise. Mr Baird took the call and came hurrying into the room. His face was grey as he looked quickly round the happy faces, his eyes searching, although he already knew he could not hope to see the one face he was looking for. In all the coming and going of the last hour, no one had noticed that Sue had not got back from her errand.

"Dad! What's wrong! What's happened?' Mrs Baird was at her husband's side in a flash.

"It's Sue. Come, Mother; we'll have to go to her."

"Sue? Where? What is it, Dad? Sit down a minute."

The young folk had all stopped speaking and the room was completely silent. Mrs Baird pulled her husband down into a chair as he tried to speak.

"I'm afraid you'll have to excuse us," he said, regaining his usual poise a little. "That was the hospital. Apparently Sue has been knocked down and they want us there right away."

"I'll get the car round."

Colin was out of the room as he spoke. The other people began to gather up their things and melt away sympathetically. Tony pushed a cup of coffee into his mother's hands.

"Drink this, Mum. It's sweet and you'll need it."

The car was at the door. Mr Baird gave a last look round and then saw that Marie was still with them.

"I'm sorry about this. We——"

Gently she cut him short in his apologies.

"Don't wait. I'm sorry, too, but I'm glad I'm here. I'll do anything I can for Mary and see that she's all right, if you'll let me."

"Mary!"

For the first time in her short life Mr Baird had forgotten Kitten in the new crisis.

"Oh, if you would; Colin will look after the others."

The house was suddenly quiet as the car drove off. Ann was hanging over the bannisters, tears streaming down her face, demanding an explanation. Marie took charge.

"If it's all right with you, Colin, I'll go and see Ann and then settle Mary. Can you get tidied up yourselves down here?"

Colin was grateful for this lead and quickly showed Marie which was Mary's room and where her things were kept. It was a help to have someone so calmly reassuring with them.

Nicholas and Ann took the news soberly. Nick vanished to his room without a word, and Colin found him there later, all his Sunday clothes neatly folded, lying dry-eyed but anxiously watching the door for anyone who would bring him news. The folded clothes spoke volumes to Colin. His little brother was an untidy monkey and this burst of tidiness was his way of sharing the family crisis. Ann clung to Marie, stranger though she was. Marie talked quietly to her and gradually the frightened little girl relaxed and was ready to try to go to sleep, if Marie promised to tell her when there was any more news of Sue.

Mary was no trouble. Marie talked to her as she helped her get to bed, and marvelled at the little girl's simple faith and trust, both in her new helper and in the Lord Jesus who, she was sure, would take great care of their beloved Sue.

Downstairs the boys had worked hard. The house was tidy and all the dishes washed and put away. Peter and Tony were persuaded to go to bed and Marie insisted on sharing Colin's vigil, at least until a call came through from the parents at the hospital. Colin made more coffee and the two sat waiting, saying little, but each knowing that the other was involved, concerned and, in the companionable silence, praying for Sue and her parents.

It was near midnight when the phone rang.

"Well?" Marie asked as Colin laid down the receiver.

"That was Dad. They've seen Sue for a minute and she is going to have an operation shortly. Dad says it's her left arm and hand that are most badly hurt. They are coming home and the hospital will phone if they are needed, and they can phone first thing in the morning. Dad says the hospital here is terrific; everyone's been so kind to them."

"Poor Sue. I'll get away now, Colin, and I'll ring in the morning, if I may."

"Of course. But wait till Dad's back, and I'll run you home."

"Not at all. It's a bright moonlight night and I know Middlebridge at all hours—no one will run off with me! Thanks all the same. Your folk will want to be alone when they get back. Tell them to let me know if I can be of any help with Mary if they both want to get to the hospital. I'm home for the next two weeks so we can surely arrange something."

"I'll tell them. That's awfully good of you, and thanks a lot for staying tonight. It made all the difference."

"I was glad to stay. Mary is a pet, isn't she?"

Colin laughed.

"She's the only one that is allowed to be a favourite and she never lets it spoil her. We all adore our Kitten."

Marie slipped away into the moonlit drive and, not long after, Colin heard the car and ran out to welcome home his anxious parents.

News of Sue's accident spread quickly through the town. Tom Hunter was the first to appear at Beechwood House on Monday morning, and when he left an hour later he took Tony and Peter with him. Graham Thompson was the next arrival. He came with a note from his mother, and left with Ann and Nicholas. Marie had phoned and when she came round later she took Mary into her care so that Mr and Mrs Baird could get peace to sleep while Sue was still coming round from the anaesthetic, in readiness to go to her as soon as the doctors gave permission. Colin busied himself quietly about the house, never far from the phone.

So the first day passed. The reports from the hospital were non-committal. Sue was 'comfortable', though Colin doubted the reality of the condition when one hand was so badly damaged that there was doubt if it could be usefully saved. Not that Sue knew that yet. Sometimes through that long day Colin found himself standing quite still, thinking. Thinking about Sue and her music, her cello, her piano. Already he had heard a few who had said, thoughtlessly and in an attempt to comfort them, 'Oh, her *left* hand', as if that was not quite so bad. But a musician such as Sue was becoming, and hoping to be, regarded both hands of equal value. How would he feel, he wondered, if it was his hand? What of his flute? He hoped he wouldn't feel bitter; he had always thought that bitterness was rather a mean reaction for a Christian to make, as if God had let one down badly, or looked the other way for a bit just when He was needed. But Colin was honest and he was pretty sure that bitterness would be hard to fight if this had happened to him. He got on with the housework grimly. He hadn't the heart to do his daily practice at the moment.

Gradually the household settled down to the new routine of school holidays and hospital visiting, answering the kind enquirers and keeping the curious as satisfied as possible. Marie was often with them, and the family discovered how many good friends they had already made in their short time in Middlebridge.

Sue lay contentedly enough. For the first day she was somewhere comfortably between unconsciousness and dreamless sleep. She was aware of warmth and the illusion of swaying but as she tried to work it out the effort was too great and she fell asleep again. It was late evening when she awoke more fully. She began to take note of her surroundings, of the nurses and doctors around her bed, of the strange apparatus at hand and the subdued voices that seemed far away. And slowly, steadily, she became aware of pain in her left hand. As the pain grew, a nurse and a doctor were at hand to help her; and as the pain receded, she seemed to sleep again, but more fitfully, with strange images to trouble her: there was a road and traffic and people and a noise and—and then she opened her eyes and saw the faces of her parents and felt again the gentle hands that kept easing her and reassuring her fears.

The first week slipped by in a round of doing what she was told, taking what she was given, eating and sleeping and having her parents often beside her. It was a week later that a careless remark further up the ward disturbed her. Sue lay in silent dismay as she tried to figure it out. So that was it. That was why they were all so amazingly kind to her. They had done all they could, but her left hand would never be much use again. And they knew her hands were the very stuff from which her career was to be made. Depression swept over her. Why? Why? Why? Why did maniacs get behind driving wheels? Why her? Why her life? Why her hand? And why on the very day she was thinking so seriously about giving her hands and her all to God? She loathed the thought that people around her were pitying her, but she lay and drank deeply at the cup of her own self-pity. If that was how God took what was going to be offered to Him, she wasn't going to make the offering. She would make a way for herself out of this. She would show people that she didn't need pity. She was young and, at the moment, she was very bitter.

Sue never let on that she had overheard the conversation about her, but her whole attitude changed. The doctors and nurses found her suddenly unco-operative. Her parents found her sulky and uncommunicative. After her first flush of determination Sue had settled to a despair; why bother? When she knew that the doctor was putting her new attitude down to normal reaction from the shock of the accident, she became harder than ever to help. And the certain knowledge that so many friends and all her family were doing all they could to help her and wish her well only infuriated her.

For four days Sue went downhill rapidly. She now lay back in bed, listless and silent. She wouldn't look at the books on her locker, barely read the cards and letters that came by every post, ate the minimum of her food and refused to talk even to her parents.

On the fifth day Miss Craig discussed the matter with her old friend, Tom.

'I want you to get a chair, Tom, and take me to Sue."

"You could never make it!" he protested. "The nearest I can take you in the car still leaves two floors to go up and about four long corridors."

"Tom, that is not worthy of you. You never stop at a few hurdles in your road. Why should I?"

Tom smiled, grimly. There was a difference but he was not going to comment on it.

"If you take me in the car and ask that nice porter at the main door to help, I'm sure we could get the use of a chair to take me to the ward. Being you," she added with an unusual flattery in her voice, "I could think we might get the use of a lift if it wasn't at a busy time."

"You win!"

Tom went off to make arrangements, and that afternoon Sue looked up to see the amazing sight of her old friend walking towards her bed, leaning on Tom

Hunter's arm. Miss Craig had refused to go into the ward in a wheelchair, thankful though she was to know it was there for the long journey through the hospital back to the car.

The invalid's face had brightened spontaneously at the surprise of seeing Miss Craig, and it was difficult to regain her new scowl in the presence of such gallant graciousness. Once he had seen his friend into a comfortable chair, greeted Sue warmly but casually, Tom withdrew, marvelling, as he so often had cause to, at the indomitable courage of the old and the frail.

"How did you get here?" Sue asked, her inate courtesy coming to her aid, making her realise that Miss Craig had made a very special effort on her account.

Miss Craig smiled that well-known twinkling smile.

"Where there's a will—you know. I just pestered Tom and we pulled hospital strings, and here I am. I don't ask much of life but when I really want something worthwhile I usually find there is a way to get it. And I was determined to visit you by hook or by crook —even if the hook had to winch me up and in through the window!"

In spite of herself Sue found she could laugh and that it helped. Ten minutes later Tom came back and Miss Craig rose stiffly to go.

"Come and see me soon, Sue," was all the parting that Miss Craig gave as she turned and waved.

Sue felt better for the visit. She lay and thought about it. It was odd, really; you would have thought that Miss Craig, of all people, would have been quick to sense her mood and her defeat, but they had only talked about being in hospital and the array of 'get-well' cards on the locker. Or had they? Nothing else had been said, certainly, but the visit itself and all that Sue knew it represented of kindness and caring, of determination and even pain to accomplish, spoke more to Sue than the most eloquent sermon ever preached.

Sue looked down at her bandaged hand. She looked past it to her injured pride, and had the grace to be ashamed.

CHAPTER NINE

SUE

Once Sue was discharged and only attending the out-patients' clinic, life for the Baird family settled down more normally. 'Normality' in the Baird household meant plenty of activity, a full programme of living and doing, and a great deal of fun. Marie and her young step-brothers were often at Beechwood House, and when they all set off for a fortnight's camping holiday the whole Richardson family came too.

They were a care-free party. Sue was sitting beside her father in the mini and had been given the task of mapping the route and navigating as they led the way. They headed north and west into the hills, revelling in the beauty of the scenery and the much-hoped-for but unexpected spell of good weather. The family were tasting a new freedom, beyond that of the ordinary holiday from school. Colin had passed all his exams well and was set for life at the academy. Sue, too, had done well and her very presence home with them again was enough to lift a load from their shoulders. That she had come home without her recent black mood meant a great deal. The others, too, had done well, and Peter, while enjoying the holidays, was counting the days to his going to the high school —not for the work of course, but for the drums and the football!

What a holiday it was. There was swimming and boating, climbing and fishing. There was sleeping out under the stars and just lazing about thinking, discussing, talking, putting the world right as only the young can. And there was music round the camp fire.

Here Sue could share with all the rest, for her hand was no disability to prevent her singing; and no one in their senses ever took a cello to camp. The real test would come later when they were home and the routine family practices took place and the band and orchestra re-formed for the new season.

It was on the last afternoon of the holiday that Sue and her father sat and talked while they watched over Mary and the camp site. The others had all gone into the town for last-minute purchases before the early start and the long journey home.

Sue saw the opportunity she had been waiting for.

"Dad, what subjects would I need to change over to this year if I don't take music?"

Mr Baird considered the question thoughtfully.

"I think it would depend on what else you had in mind," he said after a pause.

"Well, I'm not really sure. The sort of work Marie is doing really fascinates me, but I'm not quite sure that I want that as a career. I'd like to know how to help people with their problems, certainly; but I'd also like to teach, I think. I could perhaps still use some music that way, and perhaps geography, and I'd like to try R.I."

Again Mr Baird considered the matter in silence.

"Does it make sense, Dad? I don't think it's much good now taking music full time. I think the places at the top are a bit scarce and I'd rather be useable somewhere else than out of a job in a narrow field."

"Yes, Sue my dear, it makes sense. I think after we have seen Dr Barnaby again we should try and see Tom Hunter. He is very friendly with the head at school and I think we could easily get an interview with Mr Charters before the term starts and get a course worked out for you. He has spoken to Tom

Hunter about you and the accident, and I'm sure he's keen to help all he can."

"Thanks, Dad. And—there's one other thing. Since I've had the plaster off my hand, I've been wondering a lot about my cello. I know I've got to have physio. when we go back but I don't see myself playing it again, not in public anyway. Is it an awful waste to keep a big and expensive instrument like that just to have fun with at home amongst ourselves, even if I ever get that far? I mean, when people are hungry and in need, is it selfish?"

Mr Baird looked away at the far hill. Why on earth did young people have to put things so excruciatingly bluntly? He smiled and relaxed. He knew the answer to his question. Because they were so uncomplicated and uncompromising themselves. And Sue was Sue, direct, matter-of-fact and down to earth.

"Nothing is wasted, Sue, if it can be turned to good in the Master's hands. Only what we hoard to ourselves away from Him rots and rusts. Keep your cello, by all means, and remember we shall always value your contribution to our family music."

"Thanks, Dad." Sue jumped up, quickly changing the subject. "Let's take Mary for an ice-cream before the others come back. Camp will be all right for ten minutes."

She held out her strong, bronzed right hand to her father, who was still sitting on the ground. It was an old childish act and he responded to it, pretending he was rooted to the spot and then jumping to his feet beside her. In the old days he could tower above her, which was all part of the game. Now they stood side by side, shoulder level with shoulder."

Back home again, the last day of the summer holidays was spent in the feverish activity of rounding up all the books and bags and clothes needed for the new start in the morning. In the evening Sue and her father went round to the headmaster's house at his invitation, to discuss Sue's timetable for the year ahead. Colin was sitting at his belated tea, newly home from the job he had got himself for the weeks before the session at the academy would start. There was a ring at the door. Mrs Baird was upstairs getting the children to bed, and Colin went to answer it. To his intense surprise, there stood Mr Briggs.

"Good-evening. I came to—to ask—that is, to see—Sue."

Their caller seemed ill at ease and Colin tried to help him.

"Come in, sir. Dad and Sue are both out at the moment. Mum's upstairs getting the youngsters to bed but she'll be down directly."

Mr Briggs hesitated and then stepped into the front hall. He was hating every minute of this. Hating the fact that he was having to deal with Colin, hating the fact that Sue was out and he could not get over his business quickly and go, hating being in the Baird home. And yet, he could hate nothing more than he had been hating himself for weeks past.

As Colin ushered him into the study, Mr Baird and Sue arrived home.

"Oh, no!" For a second Sue held back when she heard the name of their visitor. She was unwilling to face her old trouble-maker with her recent handicap so in evidence. Then the half-forgotten memory of the grave-stone flashed into her mind and she went into the study beside her father.

For a moment there seemed to be nothing anyone wanted to say, and Mr Baird took over. Mrs Baird, who had come down at the sound of a visitor being asked in, went back to her work upstairs, Colin to his

belated tea and Sue, after a brief greeting and in
response to a look from her father, slipped away saying
something about 'taking off her coat'. For an hour
voices rose and fell dimly in the study. Later, the door
opened and the two men let themselves out of the
front door and Sue watched as her father escorted Mr
Briggs down the drive to the corner. When he
returned to the house he called Sue to the study.

"That visit concerned you, Sue, but I felt both of
you would have been embarrassed if I had called you
down. You will never need to fear trouble from Mr
Briggs again, not out of pity which I know you detest,
but because I have never seen any man so repent-
ant."

"I really came to understand him quite a bit, Dad,"
Sue said, going on to tell her father of the errand done
for Miss Craig, and of her discovery. "I was going to
ask Miss Craig about it, but she made it so plain in
such a nice way that I had been let into a very close
secret that I never asked her. And for that reason I
never told anyone, not even Colin, about it. I was
sorry for Mr Briggs but there seemed nothing I could
do except keep out of his way and not try to provoke
him in class."

Mr Baird eyed Sue critically. Mr Briggs had
mentioned his loss of wife and child and he had left
Sue's father free to say as much or as little of his affairs
as Mr Baird thought fit.

"Come and sit down. Mr Briggs told me a little
about himself and why he had been so unreasonably
unjust to you—and those are his own words, Sue. But
he came for another purpose. You see, he was driving
the car that didn't stop."

"Oh, Dad! No!"

" 'Fraid so. It was a genuine accident, but his
conscience bothered him so much about the way he

has always persuaded himself that *his* loss was due to malice—although the courts proved it was not so—that he felt sure people would accuse him of the same thing."

"Dad! Poor Mr Briggs! What a dreadful load to have carried all these weeks! You told him we never thought that for a moment, didn't you, Dad? Did you convince him?"

"I think so, in the end; but it was hard work. Such is the deadly poison of bitterness! But he is terribly upset about your hand. I think he finds it impossible to forgive himself for that."

"It wasn't his fault. I never saw him until he was on top of me, but I've always said I was day-dreaming and just stepped off the pavement without thinking or looking. Truly, I was. Besides——"

Sue stopped abruptly and bit her lip.

"Besides what?"

Mr Baird probed gently. He had seen for weeks that sooner or later Sue would have to get something off her chest. Perhaps this was the right moment.

"It was in the hospital. When I was day-dreaming that day, I was thinking about the hymn we sang at the end of the rally; you know, 'Take My Life' and I was rather condescendingly thinking I *might*—just *might* —ask God to take *my* life and *my* hands and voice. You see, I could just hear Sue Baird moving a great, hushed congregation to—oh, well, I may as well be honest and say it—tears of repentance by her wonderful music! Doesn't it sound ghastly, spelt out like that, but that's how it was. Deidre and her exhibitionism wasn't in it by comparison. Then one day I overheard about my hand and I knew people were being kind to me because they were sorry for me. That made me mad and I had the cheek to think that God had let this happen on purpose to spite me. I know now why I was so miserable—it wasn't because of the accident, it was because I no longer wanted to talk to the Lord or hear anyone pray or anything like that. I wanted to be a martyr and I wanted to believe God wouldn't have me. It was terrible while it lasted, but thank God it didn't last long."

Sue stopped and looked at her father straight in the face. These two had no secrets, or, at least, never for long. Mr Baird raised one quizzical eyebrow.

"Miss Craig?" he asked rather unnecessarily.

"Yes, the dear old lady. You know, Dad, she never said a single thing, not in words, about how I was acting and all that. It was the fact of her coming and being her that did it. I think that it was the first time I understood how marvellous it is to know God forgives our own personal sins. I've understood for years about needing the Saviour and how God's Son, Jesus, died to save us, but it was only when I knew I had something of my very own that was all wrong and that I couldn't shift out of the way that I really appreciated 'the forgiveness of sins'."

" 'Convict us of our sin, and lead to Jesus' blood' ", quoted Mr Baird half under his breath. "I sometimes think we have made the old salutary conviction of sin so much harder for ourselves by merging black and white together at the edges."

"Yes, Dad, it is hard to be sure something is wrong when you can always find plenty of people to say it isn't. But I knew blaming God was wrong, without asking anyone. He just isn't like that. I haven't hated Mr Briggs since I found out about his loss, but even if I had I would have to forgive him because I've been forgiven so much. What can we do for him?"

"Nothing much beyond being friendly. He's a lonely man even if he has largely made his own loneliness. But I'm not sure how much he will need our

actual hospitality. When he left he was going on to see
Miss Craig. I think with that breach healed they will
both enjoy many hours of happy companionship."

The new term started with a flourish. The Bairds
were no longer newcomers, and the winter pro-
grammes were soon under way with Beechwood House
the meeting place for many an extra rehearsal or club
meeting which could not be squeezed into school
hours. Sue had a new appointment for which she was
eminently suited. The committee to deal with the
rally had been asked to stay in office and they had
given Sue the task of co-ordinating all the youth
organisations whenever possible. By Christmas time
the idea was working out well and the united carol
service to be held in the town hall promised to be as
great a success as the mid-summer youth rally. Sue had
also founded, and was running, a popular library of
classical records, and from a small beginning the
innovation had snowballed into a big success.

It was on a dark December afternoon that Mr and
Mrs Baird arrived home to hear an unusual sound in
Beechwood House. As they pushed Mary and her chair
gently over the backdoor ramp that Mr Baird had
made, they stood still, listening carefully. Sue was evi-
dently home first, and alone in the deserted house she
was playing her cello. All autumn she had been cheer-
ful and busy. She took her duties with the youth
organisation committee seriously and kept everyone
linked together. She had worked hard to catch up on
new subjects in order to switch from music to teaching. She had joined both the school and church choirs
and was teaching the junior Sunday school class as
well. But she had never touched her cello and no one
ever mentioned it. Now, slowly and softly, she was
playing the air from Mozart's beautiful 'Ave Verum'
—'Jesus, Word of God Incarnate . . . Cleanse us . . .

Feed us. . . .' It was one of the items that the school choir was to sing at the end-of-term concert, and many a practice in the house had made them all familiar with its loveliness.

As her parents listened they knew that Sue had been made whole. She would not follow Colin to the academy, that they knew, but she would always make music, and good music to the glory of God, and for the fun of it and for the pleasure of those who hear and those with whom she would play. Mr and Mrs Baird stood still with bowed heads. There was only one possible response at such a moment in their lives, and that was to make the age-old, universal act of giving thanks to God for His great grace.